The Birthday Surprise

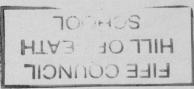
LITTLE TIGER PRESS
London

Little Monkey was very excited. It was Mummy Monkey's birthday and he had found her a juicy mango. He hid it under a bush until Mummy Monkey got back.

Little Monkey
climbed a tree to
wait for Mummy
Monkey. He had
almost reached the
top when he saw
Little Elephant.

He bounced on to Little Elephant's
head and slid down his trunk. It was
such good fun that he did it again,
and again, faster and faster until . . .

SPLAT! he landed in the bush, and he squashed Mummy Monkey's lovely ripe mango! "Don't worry," said Little Elephant. "Let's go back to the tree you picked it from." So they set off for the mango tree, but when they arrived . . .

they found someone had picked all the fruit! "Oh no!" cried Little Monkey. "I must find another mango before Mummy gets back."

Just then Little Parrot flew by.
"If you're looking for
mangoes, there's a
tree on the other side
of the river," she said.

When they reached
the river, they saw
Little Tiger splashing
around in the water.
"Have you come to
play with me?" he
asked.
"Not today," said
Little Monkey.
"We're looking for
a birthday present."

Little Elephant splashed
through the water with
Little Monkey on his back.

When they reached
the other side, they
saw the mango tree.
Little Monkey
scrambled up the tree
and picked the biggest
mango he could see.
But, as he was sliding
down again . . .

he heard an angry shout.
"That's my tree," roared a
big bad monkey. "Give me
back that mango AT ONCE!"

Little Monkey leapt on
to Little Elephant's back,
carrying the mango.
"Hurry!" shouted Little
Monkey.
Little Elephant splashed
into the river, with Little
Monkey clinging tightly
to his ears.

The big bad monkey couldn't follow
them over the water.
"That was close!" panted Little Elephant.

They hurried home through the jungle, and
Little Monkey put the heavy mango down.
But just at that moment . . .

Mummy Monkey arrived home. She was so pleased to see Little Monkey that she didn't notice the lovely ripe mango lying on the ground.

"LOOK OUT!" shouted
Little Monkey . . .

Just in time he rolled the mango to safety. "Well saved!" Mummy Monkey exclaimed. "Happy Birthday, Mummy!" said Little Monkey. "Perhaps you should eat it straightaway, before anything else happens to it!"

Written by Julie Sykes
Illustrated by Czes Pachela, based on the
characters created by Tim Warnes

LITTLE TIGER PRESS
An imprint of Magi Publications
1 The Coda Centre, 189 Munster Road, London SW6 6AW
www.littletigerpress.com
First published in Great Britain 2001
Text © 2001 Julie Sykes
Illustrations © 2001 Magi Publications
1 3 5 7 9 10 8 6 4 2